THE SHIFTY SHARK

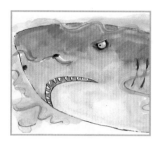

Written by
Susan Griffiths

Illustrated by
Rae Dale

HORWITZ
MARTIN
EDUCATION

Contents

Chapter 1

Eat – Or
Be Eaten!

For as long as anyone could remember, the seas off Fairtide had been teeming with fish. The warm, blue sea that lapped up against the sandy shore was full of all the things that fish needed to live long and happy lives.

Each morning, before the golden sun rose over the eastern horizon, fish around the Fairtide reef stirred, ready for the day ahead. They poked their noses out from underneath rocks or peered through the safety of the waving strands of seaweed.

"Morning, Mrs Mackerel!" murmured a large cod, as a small silvery fish darted by.

"Morning! Morning!" bubbled back the mackerel.

When the light from the rising sun filtered down
through the waves, the water became as busy as
a little town, as the fish and other sea creatures set
off in search of breakfast — or set off to stop
becoming someone else's breakfast.

Daybreak was a rush hour in the world beneath
the waves off Fairtide. It was either eat — or be
eaten!

But one morning, well before the first rays of the rising sun appeared over the horizon, something unusual in the dark sea awoke the fish.

One by one, the sea creatures sensed a large, slow-moving shape gliding past. Even in the darkness it seemed to cast a shadow over all their favourite hiding places. No-one spoke or moved for fear of being spotted.

The shape moved effortlessly through the water, a powerful tail pushing its long, sleek body with a force that buffeted many of the smaller, sleeping fish around.

This was not a shape or a shadow that any wise fish would want to investigate.

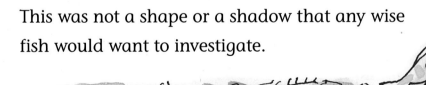

"Ouch!" cried one of the largest, brightly coloured reef fish, as he was bumped awake against a jagged rock. "Mind where you go."

"Shh!" hissed one of the other fish. "Do you want to end up as breakfast?"

The cheeky reef fish looked dopey as he tried to focus his sleepy eyes.

"What do you mean?" he yawned. "I'm the biggest fish on this reef. I'm the one who eats everyone else. No-one can catch me. Besides, it's far too early for breakfast."

The other fish's eyes swivelled nervously in his sockets. "Not for him," he said, eyeing the huge shape circling in the distance. "Not for a ... a shark!"

The reef fish gulped. The mere word 'shark' was enough to terrify just about every creature that lived in the sea. No-one liked sharks. And no-one liked sharks that had appeared, uninvited, in their neighbourhood.

"What should we do?" whispered the cheeky reef fish to anyone who would listen.

"Shh!" came back a chorus of voices. "Do nothing. Say nothing. And hope that the shark doesn't notice you. After all, you are the *largest* amongst us."

The reef fish pressed himself against the rock on which he had been bumped, and desperately tried to think of what he should do.

Should he pretend he was a piece of seaweed? That would be no good. His bright, cheeky colours would give him away instantly. Maybe he should pretend to be part of a rock.

He swivelled his wide eyes towards where the shark had last been seen. The dark sea was starting to change colour, becoming lighter, as the shimmering shape of the deadly creature slowly circled in the distance.

The reef fish screwed up his face. "As the biggest fish on the reef, I am also the smartest," he said to himself. "Besides, he doesn't seem to be moving that fast." There was no way that the sluggish grey shark moving lazily in the distance would ever be able to catch up with the quick darts and dives of a smart reef fish like himself.

The cheeky reef fish decided it would be a good idea to start the day with some fun. There was nothing like teasing a dull, grey, slow fish to put the colourful reef fish in a good mood for the rest of the day.

Quickly he flitted his brightly coloured tail, propelling himself into the open sea. A chorus of gasps broke out behind him. But the reef fish was happy to ignore them.

As he cleared his throat, a cascade of bubbles headed towards the surface.

"I say," he said loudly. The rest of the fish closed their eyes and groaned. "I say," repeated the reef fish loud enough for the distant shark to hear. "Are there any large, fat and stupid fish looking for breakfast?"

The shark continued to glide slowly through the shadows. Its cold black eyes flicked towards the reef fish, yet the direction of its huge body remained unchanged. The reef fish grew even bolder and cheekier.

"Did you know," he said to no-one in particular, "Did you know that most sharks have brains the size of a periwinkle? Imagine that," he giggled loudly.

The sluggish shark cruised closer, looking heavy and slow in the water. The cheeky reef fish made rude faces at the shark.

He couldn't believe that this poor excuse for
a fish was feared by all the other reef dwellers.
He thought it was so slow that the only fish it
would eat were those it might accidentally catch
while yawning. The reef fish giggled again, and
opened his mouth to let out another insult.

It was the last thing he would ever do.

Chapter 2

A Fearful Morning

The shark had spotted the cheeky reef fish the moment he had moved out from the rock. Instantly, his fearsome eyes flicked towards his prey.

The reef fish was right about the shark being large — but that was the only thing he was right about. The shark was neither fat nor stupid. Every centimetre of his massive, grey body was rippling with powerful muscles. And his brain was concentrating on one thing, and one thing only.

Gradually, so as not to frighten his prey, he continued to circle — but slowly, he widened his circle and drew closer to the spot where the reef fish was hovering. Moving nothing but his tail, in deliberate, careful sweeps through the water, the shark's expression remained unchanged.

"Fat, am I?" he thought to himself silently. "Stupid, am I? It's a shame you won't live long enough to learn your lesson. You may think you're the biggest — but you're really only *breakfast* for something bigger."

The circles grew wider and wider, until the reef fish was only a quick flick of the tail away from the shark's massive jaws.

"Not yet, Archie, not yet," thought the shark, lazily allowing himself to drift a little closer.

He could hear the reef fish giggling, and his cold eyes saw a trail of bubbles floating upwards. The muscles along Archie's body tensed and rippled.

Suddenly, just as the cheeky reef fish once more opened his mouth, the slow grey shark turned into a streak of liquid lightning.

Row upon row of razor-sharp teeth flashed in the dawn sunlight, and with a surge of incredible speed, Archie twisted himself up and around. In a split second, the shark's powerful jaws snapped shut!

A second later, all that was left of the reef fish was a tail, gently sinking down to the seafloor. And a trail of bubbles, still weaving their way towards the surface of the sea.

Archie smacked his rough, grey lips.

"Not bad," he said. "But not enough to really satisfy this reef's biggest, most feared predator." He allowed himself a grin which, to all the other fish hiding nearby, looked like a terrible grimace. "No-one messes with Archie."

The other reef fish shivered with fear. And then, slowly but surely, they sensed another sound coming from the west. It was a dull thud-thud. Apart from the sight of a shark, it was the one other thing that all the reef fish feared the most — the sound of an approaching fishing boat. For Mrs Mackerel, it was the last straw.

"Escape!" she shrieked, darting out from her hiding place. "Everyone to the surface!" Instantly, from behind the hundreds of rocks and masses of seaweed, a school of mackerel followed the frightened fish as she sped towards the surface. A greedy grin spread across Archie's face.

"That's more like it," he said, surveying the school of twisting and turning fish glinting in the sunlight. "Now *that's* what I call a breakfast!"

While the mackerel quickly shot towards the surface, most of the other reef fish panicked. They didn't want to be the only ones left at the same depth as the shark. Hundreds of tails and fins fluttered and thrashed their way out of the reef and into the open sea. As the mackerel reached the surface, the sea started to boil.

Immediately, the mackerel realised their mistake. They had been so busy keeping their eyes on what lay beneath them that they hadn't checked on what hovered above. The sea was now full of sharp-beaked, diving birds, crashing their way through the schools of fish, spearing one mackerel after the other. "Good morning, breakfast!" squawked the excited birds.

And through it all, the continuing thud-thud of the fishing boat's engine panicked the fish even more.

The larger fish beneath the mackerel swam helplessly in circles. Too late, they noticed a fine mesh in front of them. They wriggled and lurched from side to side. But they were also trapped — trapped in the almost invisible net that now encircled them.

"Dive back to the rocks," screamed one of the mackerel. As if as one, the school of mackerel sped through the crowded mass of bigger fish beneath.

The bigger fish wriggled wildly as they tried to escape the net that had now trapped them. But it was no use. Only the mackerel slipped through, leaving the larger fish caught, their tails flapping furiously in the net.

Beneath the chaos, Archie the grey shark grinned even wider.

"Well now that's just perfect," he said, staring at the dozens of fish trapped in the fishing net. "Now I don't even have to chase my breakfast. It's caught right here, like a great marine smorgasbord!"

One by one, he moved beneath all the fish caught in the net. With a lazy snap of his jaws, he ate every single fish, leaving only their trapped heads. When he had finally finished, he sank lazily to the bottom of the sea again.

"What a jolly good start to the day," said Archie.
"Free food all round. I do *like* this place. I think
I'll stay."

When they heard this, the remaining fish in the
seas around Fairtide realised that this was bad
news. Very bad news.

Chapter 3

A Tug Of War

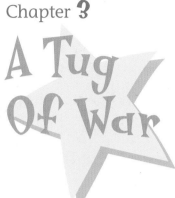

Archie spent the rest of his morning following the thud-thud of a dozen small fishing boats as they circled overhead. He had the best breakfast he had ever had, stealing helpless, trapped fish from the nets that filled the sea. This was too easy!

Once in a while Archie popped his head out of the water to see what was going on above the surface. He enjoyed the alarmed looks on the faces of the small, two-legged creatures who stood on the fishing boats, waving and pointing in his direction.

"One day," thought Archie, grinning, "I'll have you all for breakfast, too."

By the afternoon, the fishing boats had disappeared. Archie, feeling very content, drifted along near the surface, enjoying the sun on his back. With his belly full, he did nothing but circle lazily for the rest of the day, amusing himself by wondering what the small, two-legged creatures might taste like.

As the sun disappeared below the horizon, evening fell, making way for a long, dark night. Archie drifted in and out of his dreams, passing his spare time with idle thoughts. For the reef's biggest, newest fish, there was nothing to do but relax until daybreak. And then, he thought happily, it would be time for breakfast all over again. What a great life!

Suddenly, at some early hour in the dark morning, his dreaming was interrupted.

The grey shark's eyes flicked from side to side. Even though he could see nothing, he sensed something — but what was it? Slowly, he began to concentrate all his senses on trying to pick up what it was that had broken into his dream.

Soon, he heard — and felt it — again. The night sea echoed with the gentle thud-thud of an engine, slowly heading towards the reef.

"Breakfast is coming early," he said to himself.

Silently, Archie swam through the ocean towards the sound. He wanted to be in exactly the right spot when the nets came tumbling down through the water. He wanted another feast like the one he had enjoyed yesterday.

Above the surface, the two-legged creatures were talking to each other. Archie could hear the vibrations of their voices through the water.

Quietly, he circled the boat. If there were no fish caught in the net, he thought, he would eat one of the two-legged things for breakfast instead.

Archie listened as he heard the creatures rolling something heavy over the deck of their vessel. Above the water, a barrel was being lifted up and its contents poured over the side of the boat. The smelly soup gurgled and slopped as it was tipped into the sea. A fishy, stinking brown stain spread out behind the little fishing boat.

Instantly, the smell of the brown liquid reached Archie. His sleepy eyes widened in surprise.

"What is that?" he asked himself. It was the most delicious, most delectable, most desirable smell he had ever sensed.

Archie felt like he hadn't eaten for weeks. His large belly rumbled and his brain raced. He had to get some of that for breakfast. He circled quicker and closer to the surface, trying to find the source of the smell — it seemed to be all around him. The shark's mouth watered as the fishy brown liquid streamed over his teeth and through his gills.

Suddenly, something plunged through the water. Instantly, Archie's left eye swivelled and locked on to the object. That smell had made him so hungry he would eat *anything* right now.

"HA!" he cried, spotting a delicious-looking clump of fish heads slowly sinking through the water.

Immediately, he thrashed his tail and, within seconds, had clamped his huge, powerful jaws around the fish heads. Something hard and cold lodged itself in the shark's mouth. Archie shot off to the side and, with a lurch, the hard, cold thing

pulled tight and stopped him dead. It was only then that he noticed the long line trailing out behind him.

Instantly, he knew what had happened. He felt a surge of anger towards the two-legged creatures.

"Try and catch *me* for your breakfast, will you?" he bellowed in fury. "Well, I'm going to show you who is the biggest fish around this reef. I am going to eat *you* for breakfast!" Archie pulled the line through the water at an amazing speed. First he headed to the east.

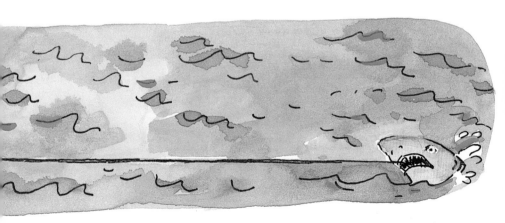

Seconds later, he swung around behind the boat. Then, he dived down and down.

"I'll tip your silly boat right over," roared Archie angrily. But once again, the line snapped tight, causing the small fishing boat to sway over to the side at an alarming angle. Meanwhile, the shark tugged the line deeper and deeper.

In his fury, Archie thrust himself through the water, first to one side of the boat then the other. His brain concentrated on pulling the two-legged creatures into the water.

He tugged downwards. He tugged sideways. He could hear the frightened voices of the creatures through the water.

"It's going east! It's diving underneath us! It's heading out west again."

No matter how hard he tried, Archie realised that he was wasting his energy. In an instant, he decided to pull the boat so far out to sea that the two-legged creatures would never be able to make it back to land.

With a determined look in his fierce eyes, he headed straight towards the source of the sunlight sparkling through the water.

Slowly, a small wave started to form around the front of the fishing boat. Archie pulled with all his might, and the helpless boat followed.

The engine of the fishing boat roared into life, and the water around the propeller thrashed white, as the motor fought to keep the boat still.

But Archie was determined and powerful. He was not going to let his breakfast escape. How dare they try to catch him! Picking up speed, he continued moving eastwards.

By midday, the sea had changed colour from blue to a deep, greeny-grey. The shark kept surging forward, dragging the helpless fishing boat behind it. Archie was in his element, surrounded by cool, deep water. His tail surged powerfully from side to side, as the force pushed him and his catch through the water.

Hours passed. The sun moved directly overhead. Still Archie and the fishing boat, tied together, continued their journey. If the fishing boat pulled one way, Archie pulled the other.

"There's no escape," he grimaced, as he kept heading eastwards. "I'm much more powerful than you are. I hope you have learned your lesson!"

The sun began moving towards the opposite horizon. More hours passed, and the light began to fade. The creatures on the fishing boat tried everything. They tried to swing the boat around, and head in the other direction. Now at full power, the engine groaned and spluttered, but still, the boat was tugged along like a toy.

Night fell as Archie felt the line tighten and pull once more on his tired jaw. But he was not going to give up. He wanted those two-legged creatures, and he would have them — for tomorrow morning's breakfast. And that was a promise!

Breakfast! At that thought, Archie realised he had not eaten anything all day. Suddenly, he felt weary, and began slowing down.

"No point in wasting any more energy," he thought. "I'll just rest until breakfast time. Then I'll strike!"

As the night drew on, both boat and shark slowly moved around each other, like two boxers trying to land a punch.

Apart from some worried-sounding whispers coming from the boat, the sea that night was calm and quiet.

At last, just when it seemed the night would never end, the first of the sun's rays dawned over the horizon. The second day of the great tug-of-war had begun.

"I'll just tow them out a few more kilometres," thought Archie. "Then, I'll leap right up and over the side. I'll smash that tiny boat into a thousand pieces and pick my breakfast out of the wreckage." He headed eastwards at great speed but surprisingly, the line grew slack. What was happening?

Archie listened carefully. The boat's engines were racing again.

Yet the boat was not pulling *against* the line —
it was *gaining* on Archie!

"Want a race, do you?" snarled Archie, streaming
through the sea like a torpedo.

Gradually the fishing boat was creeping up behind.
It rattled and shook as it tried to catch up with
Archie, who was now only a few metres in front.

Then, before Archie realised what was going on, the fishing boat whirled around and sped off in the opposite direction.

"What the … ?" started Archie. Finally, he realised what was happening, but he was moving too fast to slow down. With eyes shut, the grey shark braced himself for the shock.

Chapter **4**

A Serious Situation

Even Archie was surprised at the gigantic thrust that snapped the line tight between its two speeding ends. The force of the impact almost heaved the shark out of the water. It felt like every muscle in his body was being stretched.

And for a moment nothing happened. Archie stopped motionless in the water. The boat stood still, its engine screaming and straining.

Then, with a sickening jolt, and a noise like a train crashing, the boat lurched forward and its bow crashed into the sea again. And so did something else.

Archie felt a great weight pulling him down, down, down.

"I've got them!" he cried. "The boat is sinking!"

But Archie was wrong. Only a part of the boat was sinking — a large, heavy, steel and iron part of the boat. And it was dragging him down with it.

Immediately, Archie realised the seriousness of the situation. He would be pulled to the bottom of the sea if he didn't spit out the thing lodged in his mouth.

He wriggled anxiously, trying to dislodge the object, but it was jammed fast. Then, from out of the gloom, Archie saw something that alarmed him even more. It was the bottom of the sea, rapidly rising to greet him.

A huge cloud of sand was thrown up from the ocean bed as the winch from the fishing boat hit the bottom. Seconds later, Archie also hit the sea floor — nose first.

"Ouch!" he cried.

The force of the impact dislodged the object from Archie's mouth, and slowly he moved forward. Every muscle in his powerful body ached. And what was worse, his nose was bleeding from where he had smashed into the sea bed. A fresh trail of blood now trailed behind him.

"Ouch!" cried Archie, as he bumped into a sharp rock jutting out from the sand.

"Shh!" hissed a voice. "Do you want to end up as breakfast?" Archie looked around in surprise.

He saw a school of small grey sharks, swimming gently across the sea floor, trying to blend in with the sand. They appeared nervous.

"What do you mean?" growled Archie. "I'm the one who is looking for breakfast."

"Not today," one whispered, flicking a fin towards the deep. Then it disappeared.

Archie noticed a dark, shadowy shape slowly moving in the distance. It was massive — even more massive than Archie. But he was in such a bad mood at the loss of his two-legged breakfast, he didn't care. Whatever it was seemed far too slow and lazy to even worry about.

"That thing," snorted Archie. "It's so big and slow, it couldn't outswim a jellyfish."

"Shh!" came back a chorus of voices. "Say nothing. And hope that Great White Pointer doesn't notice you."

The shimmering shape of the Great White Pointer slowly circled in the distance.

Archie screwed up his face. The Great White Pointer wasn't moving that fast, he thought. There was no way the sluggish grey shadow circling lazily in the distance would ever catch up with him.

He cleared his throat, and a cascade of bubbles headed towards the surface.

"No-one dares to chase me!" he said loudly. The rest of the smaller sharks closed their eyes and groaned. "I'm the shark who caught an entire fishing boat, you know! Nothing scares me!"

The Great White Pointer continued to glide slowly
through the shadows. Its cold black eyes flicked
towards Archie.

Archie forgot all about his bleeding nose. He
forgot that blood in the water would drive any
shark crazy with hunger. Instead, he was in such
a bad mood, he simply concentrated on finding an
insult that would make the slow, sluggish fish in
front of him feel really stupid.

Looking heavy and slow, the Great White Pointer cruised close. Archie couldn't believe that everyone feared this poor excuse for a shark. Why, the only fish it would eat were those it might accidentally catch while yawning. It was nowhere near as fast and fearsome as Archie.

With an angry flick of his tail, he pushed his bleeding nose straight towards the Great White Pointer. Archie opened his mouth, and ...

It was the last thing Archie would ever do. He never had time to learn his lesson. Around the reef, he may have been the most fearsome shark around — but out here, in the deep, deep water, he was just somebody *else's* breakfast!